T0348658

BINGO

B	A	N	G	O
B	O	IN	G	O
A	L	★	A	N
M	IC	H	A	EL
P	A	R	KE	R

2580 Craig Rd.
Ann Arbor, MI 48103
www.dzancbooks.org

First US edition: February 2025
ISBN: 9781938603211
Interior and jacket design by Matthew Revert

Printed in the United States of America

10 9 8 7 6 5 4 3 2 1

In 1929, traveling toy salesman Edwin S. Lowe came upon a carnival game in Jacksonville, Georgia, called "Beano" that used a dozen numbers called out in random order. The winner received a Kewpie doll. When Lowe returned to New York, he adapted the game for more complicated play; he hired a retired Columbia University mathematician to devise six thousand additional numeric combinations. While testing his game at home in Brooklyn, when a friend of Lowe's accidentally yelled Bingo! instead of Beano, Lowe gave his game a new name.

Lowe was twenty when Bingo was first marketed in the 1930s. The son of an Orthodox rabbi, he also invented Yahtzee, and sold his company and the rights to his games to Milton Bradley for $26 million. Lowe became a Broadway producer and the owner of a failed hotel in Las Vegas, the Tally-Ho Inn, which expressly prohibited gambling.

Edwin S. Lowe married eight times, twice to the same woman. He died in 1986.

Bingo! Come for the fun, stay for the community.

Table of Contents

Change Your Life Bingo

Can't sing? Join a choir	Stop trying to forgive him	Foster	Stay	No blame
Sit-in at Hobby Lobby	Try someone else's God	Sandra	Fly that inner freak	Marry a person of a different ______
Walden	Use a Sorry Jar	**Listen**	No spend Mondays and Tuesdays	Substitute teach
Sandra	Tip more than the bill	Mom dies	Walk three non-contiguous countries	Don't lie
Dad dies	Don't wear a mask	Swallow a bird	Transition	Join a book club with Sandra

People in Light and Shadow

People on the television killed people on the television. In her upstairs television room, not the downstairs television room that was for the kids, Little Joanie saw a flash out the window, and she went to the window, and slid the two locks open, then slid the window up.

But she had forgotten her wine, so she went back to get her glass and then returned to the window. The night was thick in the air. She should worry about bugs, since there was no screen—so she went back again, turned off both lights, and once more went to the window.

People on the television threw bad things at other people on the television. Blue shadows jumped around the upstairs television room. It's funny/scary how a shadow can be bigger than its thing.

People on the television ran from other people on the television. There was a lot of shouting and chanting. The commentators tried to get someone on the street to comment, but it was happening too fast. People on the television wore uniforms, and then there were the homemade uniforms.

Little Joanie was Little Joanie in her family, and even in her own head, because growing up, her aunt was Big Joanie. Her ex used to call her LJ, which was okay when she loved him. She had been trying different names for a week, now that he was her ex—how strange to be divorced over the computer, and to see her ex's red face and his eyes get smaller. She had wanted to pinch his whole face closed on the screen.

So far: Joan, Joan Marie, Joan-Marie, or even go all the way with only her middle name, Marie. Make it legal.

There were lights and a fire downtown, the top floors of the taller buildings visible from her window during the day, or at night when people worked late, office lights. A siren came closer, and another siren headed the other direction, but the sounds kind of bounced, that effect.

People on the television were only on the television, click.

She liked this new guy, Tom, even though he couldn't stay the night yet because of the kids. Once she found him naked in the kitchen except for his cowboy hat, grubbing in the fridge for something to eat after sex. He had a look on his face like he had been caught stealing, or worse, but also a little proud of himself because of how he looked in his hat. She gave him a slice of leftover pizza and a glass of Pinot with an ice cube. She put a dish towel in his lap, in case of her kids.

Someone was running down the street, away from downtown. Into the sidewalk light from the streetlight, into darkness, under a tree, and then visible in another streetlight. Moving from being seen, and then not, to seen again. That was how she felt about Raymond, her ex, and Tom, the new guy—the light, the dark, the shadows. Her feelings moving.

She liked the sound of Marie. "Marie," she said out the window.

Dreaming, The Pregnant Women

The dreaming of the pregnant women began to change, the new dreams dismissed over orange juice or breakfast kimchi or chilly poi—it's the hormones, it's the result of a long confinement, it's back pain, it's an overstimulated posterior cortical hot zone. *This is so weird. I dreamed I was giving birth to a white bowl of black rice*, one pregnant woman said to another on the phone, into an old-style black phone with the little holes, and the other woman answered, *That's too cool! I dreamed I was giving birth too—mine was a square in the muddy bank of the river. A perfect square.*

A pregnant woman dreamed of giving birth to a snowball that wouldn't melt. A pregnant woman dreamed of giving birth to a song, the looping bass and drum, the singer's alto strong, rhythms going 'round. A pregnant woman dreamed of giving birth to another pregnant woman, what a lovely belly. On the news, two pregnant women, sisters living in a duplex, were interviewed: one dreamed of giving birth to peaches, the other to peach pie.

From far away, various pregnant women dreamed together of giving birth to a Pacific atoll, of dreaming face-up on the wet rocks afterward, the smooth convexity on which they lay opening their futures. One of the dreaming women was even a geologist.

A pregnant woman fell asleep in the back office of an insurance company, the ceiling fan her lullaby. She dreamed of giving birth to a kiss that everybody craved. A pregnant woman caring for her mother dreamed of caring for her father, whom she had never known. When she woke, she drew his face in the condensation on the kitchen counter, a face as round as time. Eleven pregnant women in the same pregnancy class handed on their dreams like relay runners, from one to the other—in each dream another dream being born.

The surrogate for a Polish astronaut dreamed of giving birth to a cosmological anomaly, vaguely woolly. A teenage pregnant girl dreamed of giving birth to a history book, the pages round. The pregnant president of the labor union dreamed of giving birth to the number eight, a happy number.

If the dreams were to come true, disaster. If the dreams were prophecy, catastrophe. If the dreams were a contagion but no one got hurt—a few experts thought that would be okay. And so the dreaming of the pregnant women replaced the nightmares in the headlines. No one could remember such remembering of dreams. How had the dreaming become untethered from the dreamer? Would we all meet dreaming?

The air slickens with dreams. The moon lies on its back, dreaming. The world begins again, a pregnant woman dreaming all of this, the dream a second chance.

Feti's Border Crossing Bingo

To meet my first grandson	The zipper sticks on the fanny pack	Pretend not to understand	Yes	The same grass over there
What not to admit: M.A. in Political Theory	Widowed	The bag's leaking	"Another barrier is the fundamentalism of monolingualism." - Ngũgĩ wa Thiong'o	Welcome to
The last time was in 2011	Those? I made them	**Ma'am, could you follow me, please?**	01-11-752-545-0163	Hot plane, cold hallway, hot washroom, cold waiting room
The war	My daughter and son-in-law	A nation is a map is an army	You have such a nice smile	And what were you doing in the Sudan?
No, I'm alone	Don't stand behind the white family	Memorize: 141 Sycamore Drive	They're gifts	No, I have not been to a farm in the last three months

Mrs. Nikoledes and the Motorcyclist

Living again in Athens, teaching William Blake's "The Tyger" in the American school, Mrs. Nikoledes suffers through the petulance of a high school junior doomed by his indifference. Worse, he thinks he's funny, his poetry exam reading, "Fucking, fucking, fucking, fucking trochees." Although that is pretty funny, she has to admit.

But she knows his future, because that's her awful gift—that's what made her leave Greece, and finding that she couldn't leave her future no matter where she was, made her come back. She's Ariana Nikoledes: she knows what happens to everyone. All she has to do is read the dirty, oily puddle: in the slick, there's the deadly swerve his motorbike will take, the sassy boy sliding, pinned, his bravado ground between machine and stone, his skin in shreds. She can even see the passersby.

She has a red pen, but how to correct fate? The universe has the real red pen, she thinks.

At the Cubs Game, Stella and Bella Speak Their Private Tongue

Safe!	And a Cubs birthday welcome to Stella and Bella	Fidvid bedhead	Girls, give this to the vendor	Dad tries
Fishme regular	Girls, I'll be right back	Everything's about to happen	Ridicumagic	No, she's Stella
Dad and his radio	No, I'm Stella	**Go Cubs Go**	Felt cute	Chemical nomance
Girls, do you need to	Synchogasmic	Daddy, can we have a car?	Peeeeaaauhh... nuttttts!	Sharesies, Bella
For-*nevers*	Jesus, get a hit, Alvarez	Boobdone	*Bee*-yuh *heee*-yuhh	Turning fifteen only happens once, girls

The Miniatures

Inside a cardboard box, Arthur found another miniature, number three. Who else saw? Jocko chain-smoked on the loading dock, the summer kid blabbed on her phone, D'von the soda rep scarfed sour cream chips, and the old guy stock boy flirted like a dumbass with Kacee, the cashier. Kacee wasn't ever having anything the old guy stock boy had.

This miniature wasn't the same as the first two—not a tiny factory, not a tiny farmhouse. In the cardboard box, Arthur counted seven skyscrapers, eleven yellow taxicabs, and something else, a tram or a streetcar? Was a tram a streetcar? But no miniature people. Whoever was making the miniatures didn't like people.

Nothing happened again that day. There were clouds and there was sunshine, and TV was the same. Arthur watched a superhero movie and smoked the last of his weed.

There must be miniature penises—ha!

Was it a month later? No, two: in March, at the bottom of the shopping bag, with the OJ and the Lipton's for Mom, Arthur found a grapefruit-sized ball. The ball unscrewed. Inside were two miniatures, one a town, the other a city. They fit together upside down, awesome. The city looked like it was from America, the town somewhere in Europe—he didn't know Europe enough to say. Skyscrapers and a park slid upside down into a town square with long, flat buildings and a church; the steeple fit into a sewer.

Now Arthur wanted to see all of them: he became a miniatures guy, on the hunt. He looked inside the toolbox in the garage, under the sink in the diner bathroom, in Aunt Tanya's desk, in the attic Christmas box. He liked having a purpose that was wrapped around a secret.

But they stopped. None for days, a week. It was already October, none. Long and longer. A year, then two, three. He almost forgot.

When Arthur found the next miniature, change had changed him. Other things mattered, things he had learned by changing. He cared, but it wasn't the same; Arthur thought the miniature wasn't even for him, so he put it back.

He had stopped waiting. He had gone back to school, read books. He came out. He stopped the baby stuff.

Wrong Turn Bingo

That's a funny mask	Don't back up	The other left	If I say lay down	Helicopter!
Mommy, she's very angry	Breathe	You promised	I can't	Remember that game at school?
Oh shit, eye contact	If I say hide	**Not us**	It was in the news	Mommy, is this *Star Wars*?
If I say scream	But I want to	If I say run	Oh no, we	Cars can be fixed
Double knots, okay?	Voice memo, just in case	Get off my car	He has a big hammer, Mommy	Stop that

Allison's Library Adventure

Stacks Girl from last Tuesday	Chunky beads Checkout Lady	READ BANNED BOOKS bag	She's hot	I mean it, Allison, 5:45
Cart Boy smirk	Wonder where she goes	5:45, be out front	The Rug Club's annual show	Giant cardboard Levar Burton head
Okay, Lee instead of Allison	Patchouli's disgusting	**…and she'll say, *that's my favorite too***	It's not cruising	Doc Martens shit kickers
Newspapers like wings on sticks	Kiss me, Stacks Girl	Same Gramps asleep in the kid pit	Your father won't	The best big windows
Carrying around *Cinderella Is Dead*	Don't forget, Allison	Femme	They touched hands last Tuesday	A person knows

The Dragonfly

It's 7:31 p.m. in the weird light outside a Los Angeles coffee shop, where a pizza delivery guy waits for his pickups. The city has reopened but only some, the guy's mask dangling from one ear. There are major rules now.

He's texting his sister from under an umbrella on a patio facing the parking lot. There's a dragonfly buzzing in place atop a concrete wall between the delivery guy's table and the movie theater next door. On the other side of the movie, a Pilates place he used to like, still closed or could be forever.

Slow dragonfly wings, then fast, fast.

The dragonfly moves in place and stays still, a kind of shivering. He looks the other way, where a woman at the next outdoor table tries to smile, her mask tightening. Was she really trying to smile under there? Masking a face is just like finishing the clothing thing, he thinks, like evolution. We're evolving under our masks.

It's early evening, sundown in forty minutes, and coffee's always a help for the night shift. A cup of joe, as the gross, smoggy light—pink and indigo—flattens across the horizon, dusk in LA. He's always a little unsure, this time of day. He's really sensitive to shifts in the weather. His sister's like that too.

The dragonfly's done, arcing around his table and flying off: the woman pulls down her mask to sip, and yes, she smiles. She smiled at him. It's his turn to smile back. People don't usually smile at him, he's the pizza guy, he's invisible. They think of him like they think of the weather.

The dragonfly could be the returned soul of someone—his grandfather, say. Or the woman's husband. When we know each other, we find out who's missing, which is awful, but it's helpful, but it's still awful.

No, that's wrong: a dragonfly isn't a spirit. That would be too many spirits in the world, it would get too crowded, everyone buzzing everywhere, and it would be really loud, and who could tell if someone's alive or dead.

He's a dragonfly. He's happy to be a dragonfly, just here for a moment. People move in life, delivering themselves, he thinks. Like any normal pizza guy smiling at the nice woman over there, he thinks, smiling back, nothing creepy.

After School

The good cartoons have just ended. In the brown-paneled rumpus room, a boy drapes Milo, his dog, in Christmas tinsel.

Upstairs, his sister and her girlfriend get all tangled, today and all the time: her sock, her bra, her bra, the sheet. They do this all the time, the boy knows. The boy hates his sister naked.

Trailing plastic silver, Milo the Amazing Pupster trots to the stairs, *kalump, kalump*, heading for the recycling bin again. "Tinsel, no!" the boy says to the stairs, and giggles at the idea, a dog named Tinsel.

He makes himself follow Milo, even though the girls are up there somewhere, gross, and they can make even grosser sounds, even just their giggles. In the kitchen, Milo's pawing at a tuna tin.

He points at Milo. Someone's going to have to handle that, the boy imagines saying, imitating his asshole father.

KB Meets Her Birth Mom

Early	I wish I knew	$	Lucky skirt	The tea steeps
Waiter guy, go away	*Mom, mom, mom, mom, mom*	Feelings stretchy as a piece of gum	Why?	LDS
Baby photo	Feelings spinny as a pinwheel	**The lunch**	When the past and the future don't go together	I'm at Parsons
내 딸	Same mole	Everything's symbolic	Kinda pretty	Feelings sloppy as a pile of wet leaves
Why?	You have a sister	Feelings inside feelings	Is she missing a pinky?	Thank you

The Cuellos' Thanksgiving

Children, we're selling the pharmacy	Papi yelling	W.O.W. in the basement	A turpentine smell, and then the ghost	Tammy brings José Cuervo Gold
The wind chang-ing its mind in the buttonwood tree	Garage drinking	Black-eyed Susans from the yard	"Ruben always gets the marshmallows"	Papi yelling
"Sí, soy americana"	He brings Tammy the secretary?	**Mami**	Three desserts for cousin George	A ghost? No effin' way!
The ghost has rhinestone glasses	Cowboys win!	The rooftops shimmery in oranges and reds	Damn ants in Florida	"Chica, we're not real cousins"
A ham from Antwan the mall cop	Ruben and Esther on clean up	The ghost is so pro-Castro	"I'll drive Tammy home"	The O.G.s bitch the most

Unemployment Benefits

I was fired from my job as a soda jerk for wandering away from the milkshake machine, the milkshake machine making a grinding roar that matched a sound in me. I was fired by a bookie for revealing my real name to a bettor. I was fired by the Italian restaurant in Windsor, Ontario, because I was not Canadian, and I was using my lover's social insurance number illegally, and I guess no one wanted my retirement contributions to be hers in sixty years. This was before the Eighth Wave of Regret.

Just after the Thirteenth Wave of Regret, I was fired for drifting off too often into a fugue state, a low-oxygen spiritual environment where a version of me always seems to be hammering a piece of iron and trying to catch the sparks in his hand while singing. I would go there unaccountably: I would be swimming, and I would not be swimming. I would be lifeguarding, and no one would be safe. No one else was ever there, which was okay, but I would go there when I was supposed to be doing a job. So I kept getting fired, hired, fired.

Nineteen Waves of Regret later, I was still trying to catch the sparks. I would try to describe them to my lover: they are fireflies, but no; they are like the bits of jalapeño in the cornbread, no; they are the sudden untranslated Japanese word in a sentence, no. It is true, however, that the sparks can be felt with the tongue. And sometimes in my lover's mouth.

I was fired for reading in the bookstore when I should have been dusting spines. I was fired for Benito doing coke but everyone was fired. That was at another ice cream place, where we the busboys spent our shifts ambushing one another: fudge on the handle of the pressure washer, dish soap on the floor, maraschino cherries squashed inside a shirt, quarters glued to tabletops.

I was fired by the assistant manager at Bohack's supermarket, a guy who died of an aneurysm a year later, at twenty-five. He already had an eye that rolled off and to the left, above his ear, especially when he was yelling at me for jamming the cardboard baler. Don't mention his eye, the Big Boss said, and I was sorry, but I wasn't really there: the hammering and the sparks, in me, were there.

Is my being me an excuse? My lover says yes. Forty-three Waves of Regret. Fifty-seven Waves of Regret.

What happens if the world that feeds me isn't the world I need?

I was fired by Julio, one of three Julios who worked at the country club. My job: towel distribution, soap refilling, empty glass pickup, stacking collapsible chairs into a wooden bin, patrolling the driving range for empties. My real job: Sixty-three Waves of Regret, and standing in place in a moving world, the sparks in me like meteors going the wrong way.

Dr. Ozan Builds a Violin

A little hope each morning	Clayre won't step into his workshop	Balkan maple, spruce, plywood, pear, ebony	Once will be enough	In their marriage, Clayre & Ozan have broken a few strings
Dreamed a tree with chinrests for leaves	Miter into a bee sting	"A sandwich and a cup of coffee, and then off to violin-land." -Sir Arthur Conan Doyle	Peg drill	Menuhin's Guarneri, "The Lord Wilton"
Clayre started playing again during Covid	The asymmetrical f-hole	**Self-portrait of a retired ophthalmologist**	Inevitably, failure	Varnish
Narex gouge	KUOW, Puget Sound Public Radio	Glue, glue, glue	YouTube	If only to handle the wondrous tools
"Music is not illusion, but revelation rather." -Pyotr Ilyich Tchaikovsky	He finally stopped driving by the office	Clayre has her tennis	But the humidity in the Pacific Northwest	"It doesn't have to be great, hon"

First Day Bingo

The blue pen, the Post-Its, the paper clips, the other Post-Its	Dream in which you can only meow	Your boss, not your dad	One POC	College hookup is a coworker
Freedom is the opposite of Time	They'll know	The red pen, the Post-Its, the stapler, the other Post-Its	Dream in which your new boss melts	Everyone can tell
How early won't feel late?	Wrong charger	**Lunch**	*How to Succeed at Being You Without Knowing Who You Are*	Mom's doctor calls
Dream in which your arm and hand are goo	Fjörlen's Syndrome	"Where did you go to school?"	The difference between responsibility and guilt	Catholic school kids jam the bus
Return home to check the stove	The Apocalypse	Shouldn't have slept with the window open	Bits of dreams	Of course, today

The Plumber

If only to be a member of the secret society, to know the handshake, to understand what the double knots in the bandana meant, to understand the personalized license plates. Lewis Jr. has never been in an in club, and this was the innest. According to Lewis Sr., the club had a newsletter that arrived by email and then erased itself when read; according to Aunt Marge, they were knowable in distinct arrangements of flowers, when one saggy tulip faces east. According to Uncle Ray, the hand gestures of the dispatch clerk were code, and the preacher's sermon was always about something else.

Regular people couldn't tell, but the Vedder family knew. That made them members of a different kind of in club, even though none was in the in club.

There had to be a centralized shadow organization, and a leader. But there couldn't be a list, since a list could be found and read by someone, or there could be a leak, and then, no secret. They don't make simple mistakes, Aunt Marge said. Still, there had to be a gatekeeper, right?—so anonymous that non-members could never guess who. The solution might be to identify that person, and then approach, but don't blow it. That's what Lewis Jr. thought.

More thinking: in what profession would Lewis Jr. meet a lot of people, have access to their lives, and ultimately be able to figure out how to make his approach? Flight attendant, manager at Starbucks, police officer, nurse…the access wasn't enough. He needed to be socially nimble, to climb up and down the social ladder, and do so without being seen. So Lewis Jr. became a plumber, meeting people in their homes.

Lewis Jr. was confident he would know when he would know. So he had to stay ready.

When it came to staying ready, love was out, of course. That's why he didn't fall in love with Allison when it seemed possible. A man had to be free. If only she had been in the secret society, and had told him so that night. But he couldn't ask her, and that was that.

Nine years as a plumber, Lewis Jr. still waiting for a sign, fixing the leak in the Magnersons' bathroom, crawling around on his kneepads. Not in the club. Was it ever even possible? Lewis Jr. admits to wondering, reaching for a pipe threader.

How Phil Imagines the Afterlife

1. Would you have a couple of bucks for the kid with the Mai Tais? I asked him to go easy on the lime.
2. I like how the umbrellas from the two umbrella rental companies mix together, the red-and-yellow and the green-and-purple. It all looks so planned, combining the colors that don't go. It's like fashion from when I was a kid.
3. Your shoulders are burning. Here.
4. Did you remember to freeze the bottles of water?
5. Stop doing that, you're getting sand on me.
6. Don't you love that the ocean's got so much rhythm? All of those wild creatures—and they're hunting each other inside that big rhythm.
7. I'm not sure what to say about it all, I know it's just the ocean, but I love the size of everything inside of everything. I mean, the stuff in the stuff. How much is going on under there.
8. That could be Europe.
9. So I was thinking, I'd like to get to know Sam. I don't think I've given him much of a chance.
10. Did we set up too close? If we stay too long, we'll need to move higher.
11. Music from bad neighbors. Cigarette smoke.

12. Other people, man.
13. Being okay with not being okay, and being okay with this being it.
14. I'm going in the water. When the kid comes, will you handle it?
15. That doesn't look healthy.
16. Did you bring the cord for my sunglasses? I'm going to try wearing them on the air mattress.
17. Did you make the reservation?
18. I guess it's okay that the lifeguard's a teenager.
19. The tide is on a schedule, but the weather isn't.
20. I brought this book from the house. Check out all of these names: bladderwrack, pulse, forest kelp, gutweed, Scotch bonnet, mermaid's purse, common cup, lace cup, spiderwood, sponge wood. A name is yours, even if you're a thing.
21. Did you ever think about that? I mean, lives just happen overnight, and then they wash up here.
22. Like us.
23. When the Mai Tais arrive, let's toast. To the next adventure.

Long Marriage Bingo

Sorry (not)	Where did you put my	Getting a gift right	Horny	Only a few secrets
Okay, let's	No blame	Behind the left ear with the tip of a finger	Blame	It's okay
I've got it	Not the purple one	**Love**	I gave you that scar	Thanks
Never saying "My mom was right"	I gasp when you cut your finger	You're in a room even when you've gone	Which time was that?	Without asking
Dinner in five	So it's only a cough?	Stopping just short. Starting again. Stopping. Now.	You tell it	Sorry (really)

Grandma Challenges Nurse Pamela to a Footrace

They agree the race will start at the nurses' station, the widest part of the hall on Three, and that Nurse Pamela will walk backward, and she's not allowed to speed up, and that Grandma can call stop at any time and take a break. The finish line will be the double doors to the elevator.

Nurse Marco takes a piece of paper from the printer and uses his favorite scheduling highlighter to make a sign, NASCAR GRANDMA, which he tapes to the front of her walker, and he cuts up a couple of ads from *Senior Women's Health* and tapes them to the sides of the walker too. "Sponsors, hah," he says to Nurse Jae, who's new, and she laughs too.

All of the rooms on Three have visitors' chairs the staff moves to the doorways, so that everyone who's able can watch.

The morning of, Grandma has a long conversation with Nurse Marco about whether to wear slippers or grippy socks, as Nurse Marco gives Grandma's bad calf a massage.

All the rooms on Three have fresh flowers, what the nice people at Fili Flower can't sell and would throw out, and their nice boy brings on Sunday afternoons. This week, carnations and orange lilies.

The right wheel on Grandma's walker tends to wobble if she tries to go fast, but the left wheel's true. Nurse Marco might be able to fix that.

Grandma asks Nurse Marco if his parents are alive. It's a sudden question in the middle of the leg massage, and he stops and looks up at her—she has such an expression on her face, with the one droopy eye that gets a little leaky, the skin under the eye thin and raw—and he answers, "My mother. In Guatemala."

Grandma nods, "Yes. I can tell." Which might mean nothing, or it's affection.

There's discussion at the nurses' station about Grandma's "feistiness." There are nurses who believe that people become their true selves as they age, settling into their real personalities, but other nurses believe that when a person has been left alone in life, loneliness warps who they are. The conversation started with a magazine story. Adele, the social worker, left the magazine open to the article on the table in the break room, next to the thank-you donuts from Mrs. Johnson's son.

In her patient history, Grandma has been written up for throwing things—although never at a caregiver or a visitor, only on the floor or away from her bed, and that's very important. If she were a risk to others, instructions would need to be added to her chart, a blue sticky, and she would not be permitted memorabilia in reach. Patients on Three rely on touching their old things.

Grandma's primary and the OT have encouraged Grandma to be more active. That's the source of the footrace, Nurse Pamela pushing Grandma to get out of bed more often, to walk with her walker, and Grandma responding. "Oh, now. I could beat *you* in a race."

She has a name, of course, but she prefers Grandma. Nurse Pamela sometimes calls Grandma by her name, because Nurse Pamela's a pip, but also being irritated can be good for rehab, and some patients do better when they're put in competitive situations.

At the nurses' station, the question arises whether a patient whose character has become "more focused," as Nurse Meli says with air quotes, can be changed. When an older person becomes their true self, how can we tell it's true? Nurse Jae says that in her religion, we have many true selves. The other nurses don't know what to make of this.

It's hard to be a nurse. Covid took so many. The nurses' compassion for their patients is both professional and personal, naturally, and yet they have to compartmentalize, to feel their own futures will be different, largely due to their experiences as nurses. They will know better—that's the hope, at least. The nurses overwhelmingly believe that the third floor is not their own future, a necessary belief for those who work on Three.

There's a sheet cake in the break room fridge for Manny O'Connor's eighty-seventh—he's changing pretty quickly now. There's agreement that he would share if he could understand, so the sheet cake will be served after the footrace.

When Grandma is ready, the spectators settle in their chairs, the nurses all here—they timed the race for shift change, so that Day and Night could all attend—and Nurse Pamela puts Nurse Marco's bike helmet on Grandma.

Time changes how everyone feels, but even though some of the attendees have simply lived longer, their feelings stopped changing. For some, their feelings have become too big for their worldly bodies, they're getting ready to go. That's what the nurses think. Grandma's the question, though, the one they talk about most in the break room, because she's flippy-floppy about her own death.

The race is rigged, unfair, Grandma has to win, because that's what Three needs, where winning doesn't happen.

People Floating Away Bingo

No shoelaces!	Aunt Sarah's outlived three husbands	Quick, hook it on her belt	Only since the big rain	Aunt Sarah's compression sock, floating
Look, Barry has contrails	Do they go to the same place?	Usually at dusk	Try the ladder	Can they steer?
What the hell?	The Mixon twins	**Hold on, we're coming**	Why Sarah? Why not us?	Even bratty Oscar
Aunt Sarah made a mean chicken soup	Rashid empties his pockets	A bicycle left in a parking lot	Jump	Everyone to the upstairs windows
Why none on Mondays?	*Bang bang bang* until the window opens	Weights in boots	When is it scary?	They don't wave back

Mickey Falls Asleep at Work

That was so late for a Tuesday	Don't text her	One sock	Did she really shout "Bingo"?	Q3 due Monday
That 3rd Johnny Walker Black	"Fruit dreams belie sexual vulnerability" - Dr. Mehta Singh	When the dick swipes right	Kissing in the Uber	"Dream lover come rescue me (yeah)" - Mariah Carey
Excel is kind of Bingo	**strawberries**		Cutler a douche in the elevator this morning	Not a big fruit guy
		I love hockey too!	"The body dreams in adolescent causality" - Dr. Arvina Hoolse	It was so hot when she
		No, not a dog walker—what a cliché—I'm a veterinarian	3 Daiquiris	Twice

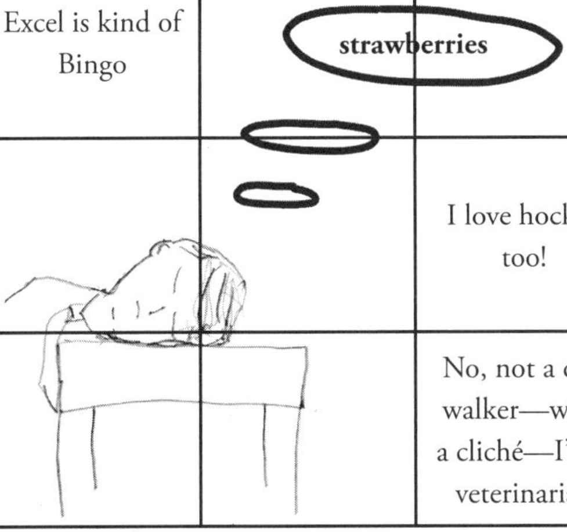

The Strangeness of Knowledge

On a bus to Des Moines to help her sister, a woman unwraps her dinner, cheese and lettuce on soft bread (dental work), an orange for after. The surprising food smells and the crinkly sounds of the wax paper, small sounds, combine in the tight bus air. Outside, heavy wheels on the road, the rush of light traffic, travel metronomes, rhythms to sleep by. Until the window darkens, and in the conical glow of her personal reading lamp, the woman's reflection comes into focus, riding along in a feeling like privacy.

Can the same smell be different to someone else? That seems chemically unlikely.

The teenage girl stirs in her earbuds across the aisle. The girl's stomach grumbles.

The seconds repeat, three or four of the same, and then different small events occur for three or four seconds, nothing intelligible. How experiences become other experiences: wheels as music, music as echo, rhythm as memory, feelings as sounds, a woman on a bus thinking about her sister.

Over the cornfields, the road a taut, shimmering, lost future, bats swoop in illegible routes, night scribblers. The woman studies her reflection, but not fully: she's too close to the glass, and the bats and the intermittent lights interrupt from out there, as the difference between a life and what's outside meet in her image. But then she's too close, too transparent, too solid, which add up to disappearing.

The teen opens her eyes, a look. The woman understands, says, "Here," and offers half a sandwich. The girl smiles. The woman smiles back, hers a little sore.

High School Reunion Bingo

<table>
<tr><td>No Dolores</td><td>Now I remember why</td><td>MC says “rad”</td><td>Time pooling at the bottom of the mind</td><td>Salmon or pasta</td></tr>
<tr><td>Hottie was a band kid</td><td>Where’s Dolores?</td><td>A bully is a bully is a bully is</td><td>Time accessoriz-es the soul</td><td>I’m a large animal groomer</td></tr>
<tr><td>Even with the Driver’s Ed teacher</td><td>Time not the camera but the flash</td><td>Regrets</td><td>That guy’s a Trumper?</td><td>Would Mindy know about Dolores?</td></tr>
<tr><td>He brings the girlfriend he met abroad</td><td>Dolores, that kiss</td><td>How is this possible?</td><td>Dolores, alone in JoBurg, I saw</td><td>The way time flattens the soul, old seltzer</td></tr>
<tr><td>Time’s a soul pudding</td><td>I’m in dental forecasting</td><td>Dolores, I sleep with a pebble under my tongue</td><td>I wouldn’t be here, but</td><td>Weed</td></tr>
</table>

Ruhi's Bathroom Bingo

<table>
<tr><td>Well, the universe is unfair, so</td><td>Meena put it in my bag, Mom</td><td>IYKYK</td><td>Who decides what's wrong</td><td>"To steal is to give away one's self."

-Gandhi or someone</td></tr>
<tr><td>Sing a little in the mirror</td><td>The store tags WON'T COME OFF</td><td>Just a minute</td><td>Is that a zit?</td><td>Want</td></tr>
<tr><td>Meena keeps a lookout</td><td>Greed</td><td>I dare you</td><td>No cameras in the bathrooms</td><td>Meena won't herself, obvi</td></tr>
<tr><td>But they're pretty</td><td>Ocupado!</td><td>Ever since Randi in ninth grade, Meena</td><td>3 tops at once is 🔥🔥🔥</td><td>Like six cents an hour</td></tr>
<tr><td>You always say no, Mom</td><td>An 'A' in US Gov</td><td>S, M, L</td><td>Don't cry</td><td>When being underage works, for once</td></tr>
</table>

People Everywhere Are Having Sex

In her aunt's pantry. In a camper during a thunderstorm, now that's got to be something. In the TV room as soon as the grown-ups go out. After clubbing, tired. At the movies, having waited for the usher to clean, giggling because it's funny to try being quiet. At the high school musical during half, sneaking off to the science lab, in the dark with those big black tables with the hooped spigots, like Reapers in that Xbox game. In his stepmother's Audi, of course, a kind of spite, windows closed, to smell it up. Right now, everyone's doing it on airplanes all over the sky.

Being a teenager is having a new body, and she likes it. And seeing everyone's body wherever she looks.

First thing in the restaurant, Shahid asks Tracy, *How about it?* Tracy had only just sat down, and she really wants a coffee, and Shahid used to be the boy who would order for her—and there it would be, coffee and lots of cream, three sugars. Why did it always have to be the guy who starts? Tracy doesn't understand. She's just as guilty, though. Guilty as in horny.

But this time when they texted about something else, nothing, she asked, *Where do ppl have sex in bathrooms? I want to* And then the game was on, she had started it this time, the flirting back and forth, the tingly hairs on her neck, a little bit of pit sweat, and of course, down there. Him knowing better than to send an eggplant.

But getting to the restaurant through the rain, and the delay on the bus, even though the bus is free with her card, and her feet wet, her tights sagging, some dude too close to her at Warren and Fifth, skeevy, not cool, and Shahid not ordering her coffee. The feels shrink. Even though showing up is saying yes.

Did you check it out? Tracy nods toward the RESTROOMS sign by the kitchen. The waiters are busy enough.
It's shady, you go through a lobby to a hotel.
A hotel?
Yeah, back there, it's through and back there. He gives her that smile. *Cool?*
Cool, she says. *You first, then wait, I'll be a minute,* she says. Since it's just sex, and it's fun even when it's not, and even better when she's in charge.

César's Eye Exam

Warning signs	$800 for the Tom Hardy frames	Hate this	Mom's blindness, at the end	Always better things to do
"When I see, my body becomes the whole world." -Aarhuis Nomo	Let's go retro '70s	There's being gay and then there's gay	Different eyewear in a red state	Why is the soul blurry?
Hate this	How much? What?	**X R 6 L T** **Z F L P 4** **5 D M 3**	No, you're old	Not a single cute guy on a poster
Does everyone's twenties ruin their forties?	Gay blind isn't a thing, Mom	Dr. Singh, what are those glittery things?	"It's fun seeing my name on someone's ass." -Versace	To Mom, "light" meant "God"
Bad job #23: eyedrops nurse	Hey, Siri, what do you see?	Mom began with cataracts	Lite jazz sucks	Frogurt as a reward

Doug and Linda's Orgasm Diary

At your dad's	Under the table when	Then Shellie's Frenchies started to howl	I love you, Dougie Dog	Rule #11: no cemeteries
"For everyone this little book might help"	Ouch	Five hula hoops	You were asleep	Were the cops still upstairs?
Spatula	Can you imagine some people never	**Did you?**	When your sister walked in	Iowa City
I love you, Linda Shminda Winda	Boise	Remember, we had to wait for	Arrows, motion	I wish
The Thing	Christ, you left it where?	Oven mitts	You forgot the	No, you don't have my permission to

Sara Rosen Sees Cyndi Lauper at the Walgreens

Jesus, that's her	Movie idea: Walgreens Musical	Is that Liza Minelli?	"Fate is for the weak." - Mom	Okay, this once, get the Dior eyeliner
Those lips, the hair— not Liza	Girls just	What's the Rx for love, Cyndi?	Without asking, a picture's rude	Viv's ringtone
Is that flypaper? Eww	Viv, pick up	**That can't be her**	Viv, she bought	"I'd like to be a queen of people's hearts." - Princess Diana
On Molly with Viv, singing "She Bop"	Everyone is too young	Movie idea: Cyndi imagines seeing Liza at the Walgreens	Put back the retinol	Wrong high-tops
Got2b Bleached Ultra Platinum	A so much better Gwen Stefani	Viv, you won't	If living upstate, this wouldn't	Movie idea: steal Cyndi's wallet

Delilah Hates Chem

H_2SO_4	Pretend not to understand	It's on, Ms. Stagnitta	A tampon for Jamie	What if poison and eyes bleed
Dead people are sad	That boy in the student store, yum	Changing one person's mind, each of us, then the whole world	Ms. Stagnitta pees in a sink	Amal Clooney went to NYU Law
How to make Special K	What if bees fly out all the vents	**Hello, Delilah? Are you paying attention?**	10 KNO3 + 3 S + 8 C	Mmm, sex
Law school sounds cool	Flo doesn't shave, total hero	What if terrorists	Ms. Stagnitta can suck Axe	Why have a phone that's off
What if a penis	Not cool, Staggs, busting out Spanglish to someone Latinx	That girl at Trinh's house party, yum	CH_3COOH	That's a hard no to transphobia, Gretchen

Ireni and the Ghost

1.

The lights in the living room weren't flickering, more like *zzztsssing*, the sound of the hairspray Grandma Cora would spray on Ireni's hair. But not that sound exactly. Being precise about what the lights were doing would matter later, Ireni could tell, when she would tell Louis. There was a ghost *right there,* and Ireni needed to remember everything. But she couldn't actually say what the lights were doing; there was no way she knew to identify what was happening, she had no context for this, and that's also how Ireni knew it must be a ghost, because a ghost is what's left alive when the things you know end. After knowledge, that's where the unknown is, right?

Ireni tried to turn off the lights, but of course that didn't work. The switch went flippy, up and down like a dislocated finger, loose and clicking a little, yuck. The lights seemed aware. The ghost was in charge of everything.

She felt like the ghost meant well, for a ghost.

Being in a room with the lights on can feel like being tied up in a web of yellow strings, like being caught in a big invisibly knitted scarf. Ireni wasn't a knitter, more go-go-go-go, as Louis said once when they went hiking, and he saw her relief to be outside again. She works at the Conservancy for a reason, Louis.

Back home together, she would often step a few steps behind Louis and turn off the lights after he left a room. He knew she did this. He thought Ireni was being careful with their money, that it was political too, because she was very political compared to him, and she let him think that, but it was more about feelings.

"Hello?" Ireni says.

"Hello," says the ghost, and the words are yellow and electric. Not spelled in the air but in the air too.

Okay, that's a lot, Ireni thinks.

"Who are you?"

"I'm you."

"Louis!" she yells. "LOOOOUIIIIISS!"

2.

Grandma Cora used to say make two decisions every morning, one for today and one for next week. That's what Ireni planned to say at the funeral tomorrow, because quoting a dead person's wisdom is how we continue their lives. How we keep them alive.

No, that's not right. Wrong, just like that advice on www.eulogy.com about telling a cute story that's a little embarrassing, which wouldn't have suited Grandma Cora, and it definitely wouldn't be Ireni's preference to stand there and turn red on purpose. She hates being embarrassed.

What's the difference between a decision made for today and a decision made for next week? Every morning, you're supposed to know enough about next week to make a decision? Ireni should have asked Grandma Cora before she died—before she couldn't make any more decisions about next week.

The Conservancy crowd would be at the funeral, and the poll workers she's met at First Baptist, most folks who know her knowing how Ireni was raised, and the remaining friends from Grandma Cora's union days, and probably the hospice nurse. Being secretary of the Garment Workers' isn't writing things down, Grandma Cora once told Ireni, and laughed. Ireni writes that down, which almost makes her smile, but she's too teary.

Outside, the snow's already six, eight inches. Larger drifts, at least a foot, fold up and pile against the south sides of things, and it's all a big damn cake. Grandma Cora needs to jump out of the cake, because she did that too in the sixties, like in another of her wild stories, and not be dead.

"Reni?" Louis calls from the den.

"Mmm?"

"You might want to check the weather. Did the funeral home say anything about weather?"

"Mmhm."

Ireni turns from the kitchen window and goes into the mud room. She puts on her boots, Grandma Cora's down jacket, a thrifted Detroit Lions scarf, and a pair of lined mittens. She's been wearing Grandma Cora's gold chain for a month now.

Louis the Loser, that's what Grandma Cora called him. She was right. He never gets off the fucking couch. He of course didn't check the weather.

Ireni steps out back and into the snow.

It's the same ghost as last time, only this time it's a bird.

This time the air's perfect.

Ireni stays calm. "You," she says.

The bird sits on a frosted branch and doesn't answer. But then Ireni hears it sort of, in her head, say, "Us."

"What does that mean? Jesus." Ireni doesn't know what else to say. "Did Cora send you?"

"When I died," the bird says in its way, without words, "I saw our future. Believe in something," the bird adds.

There's a fluff of white on the bird's head, a brownish crown, and her wings are tipped in orange. She's like the end of a paintbrush, and all that snow is what she painted.

"Cora?" Ireni says. "Is this a message? Have you seen Cora?"

"Being alive is just one way of being alive," the bird-ghost kind of says.

3.

Ireni is ready. She has a go-bag packed, nothing Louis will miss, and he won't miss her either after a while, she's pretty sure. She could go have a baby in the woods, if she were pregnant, or even flee the country, he'll just live his life.

It's Saturday, it's March, and the snow's melting. Cora's been dead nine days. The funeral was Monday, and people stopped coming to the house Thursday, nice people, but that's enough.

As though into a carwash of beauty all around her, sudsy snow melting and dripping, the world waiting for her, Ireni picks up her go-bag and steps outside at last.

It's like stepping into a whole ghost, being inside the outside in a big rinse.

Bye, Louis.

Car Crash Bingo

That wasn't there before	DUI	A dozen men step from the woods in military gear	After therapy, no tissues	Hot tomato soup
The blurred result of your spiritual unease	Bad driver	Texting Jill	Python	Protestors
Opportunity: ex steps off the curb	Jill butt dials	**Fate**	So much blue, who knew?	Three state troopers speeding the other way
Imagining a bag of alive things	Rihanna's "Shut Up and Drive"	DUI	Projectiles	That pickup should be nicer
Heading home from NASCAR	Jill can't know how much she hurt you	Last night's so-so pasta	If an ambulance can go that fast	A different excuse than last time

Birthday Shopping Bingo

Quick, he's coming, close the browser	Can I give him a sex toy?	Could be Hank's not the one	That looks real	Everyone needs secrets
Clickbait	No return policy	Check his browsing history for something fun	Which tab was that?	I could do this with Jimmy
4.3	"For Women" is the best	**My Cart**	Want, need, cost, value, fun, use, want	To feel
So many misspellings	Will it say "sex toy" on the package?	Practice aloud: *For this to work long-term, Hank, I need you to be willing*	I wouldn't be offended, no	Life's the sale that's always ending
Could be Hank's the one	Durability rating	Some Russian who knows everything about me	His credit card	I'll keep it at my place

Janet and Her Soul

Some people can be what they want, Janet thinks, jealously, at the mall. They can be beasts, they can give in, their beastliness okay. They're in their lairs and then they come out to hunt, and they feed, and they send a scout ahead of the horde, and the other beasts on the other side of the river (the mall has a fountain) make beast noises, and the hordes side-eye each other or flat-out stare down. Packs of beasts shopping, she thinks. Picking up provisions for the journey ahead.

Janet is here to get a pair of earrings for her soul, to accessorize; she's meeting Elsa in the food court. Because a soul has moods, and times of day it wants to be at the mall, and colors, and for sure a soul needs to be kissed, and to kiss. Janet's soul is a Spring.

Janet believes in the soul, being the great Greek philosopher she is, what Ms. Daniels called her the other day in Language Arts class, Ms. Daniels and her jokes, Janet's parents are from Indiana.

Who's more lonely, she thinks, a soul, a Greek philosopher, or Ms. Daniels? It's like Fuck, Marry, Kill, only not.

A roving band of beasts has reached The Gap, and they're turning around, almost all eleventh-graders, most she knows. They're aiming this way. She should have picked an exit strategy, not just Starbucks as a goal.

The mall is also *Fight Club*, Janet thinks. Starbucks is also a standardized test. The mall's just a racetrack, everyone driving around with ads on them. Like Elsa said in Bio the other day, "Who needs The Gap when you have H&M?"

But sometimes a soul needs to go shopping, so watch out, Western civilization. All of the feelings in her own body ready to be freed, all of the peoples around the world ready to be freed, her ship will be waiting for her at the end of the day, i.e. Parking Lot 3. Queen Janet is here, my people, and I love each of you in your humanity.

But first Janet needs to be unseen, to slip past the invaders and the beasts and the haters, the older kids, what she wants to be. She hides in the bathroom, feet up on the toilet, in case anyone peeks under. Her soul in a tight, tight ball. Tighter.

Speculative Fiction

He spent his twenties the star of a bad novel. How strange, and unworldly, to age that way, his twenties like another planet. While the sun did a slow roll in those dimly lit years.

Was he a hero? He couldn't tell. Just because everyone looked oppressed, and there were bar scenes and wingmen, which made him feel like a hero—was that any kind of proof?

In an early scene, there was a promising opportunity to linger with a lover who might be more than just a dalliance—but he needed to leave, time and space his ready excuse, a man in the pull of the planets. Stupid, sure, because the lover was amazing, but the story he told he believed enough to tell.

In one scene, he acquired a friend. In another scene, he got in an Uber, and there was a cat in a shoebox, and the Uber woman gave him the cat, and so he had a cat. The cat was a girl he named Fireball, a sidekick name, but the cat lived on another planet too, because that's a cat.

And the more he drifted toward his future, the more Fireball lived alone, the way a cat does, walking the countertops and the windowsills all night, a night terror unto itself.

In another scene, he could have left. Opportunity and risk. Values he didn't understand defining him.

Regrets followed. When he became desperate, he regretted not leaving. Lesser opportunities, more regrets. People.

In one scene, he was shaving, and singing into the mirror, when someone was hurt in the courtyard.

In one scene, there was a new lover who stayed. Fireball didn't like the new lover, and the cat would piss on the lover's clothing overnight. He had to make a case for his cat as an independent being and not an extension of himself, not an indicator of his feelings. That didn't go well.

Toward the end of his twenties, too many scenes were the same. Was that science too? Data? Fantasy? He began to want out, off-world, to change his name, to be anonymous differently.

In a late scene, he stood and faced a cloud-swept moon from the rooftop of his building, and he could see the potential of a life beyond his own. So he made a decision. He gave Fireball to his neighbor, the single mom with the badly behaved terrier. Consequences? Not when a man walks away.

Sure, he made himself ignore the problem in the woman's apartment, the dog and the cat antagonists, and her son, his sometime friend, who would grow up into violence. But think of it as comedy.

Greek Diner Coffee Bingo

All the new lovers	"Coffee makes us severe, and grave, and philosophical." -Jonathan Swift	The jingling lingo of the cooks and the tinkling of spoons	I had fun last night	Check out that sweater
I liked it when you	Aphrodite hailing a cab, shaking off her umbrella	A misbuttoned top	A mind and its steamy windows	Someone's wallet
The new lover makes cute faces at the kid	Soccer on TV	**Free refills**	The hunter chases the stag around the cup. Life chasing death or vice versa?	Sorry, it's my mom. I have to take this
Let's both sit on this side	Athena in the next booth, her armor made from the skin of a Giant	*Kalimera!*	Is there something you'd like to do this afternoon?	You've got a little...no...to the left.... Here, let me…
Yes, but I've got a busy week	So it's only a cough?	Silence or thoughtfulness or nothing to say?	I'm so glad Suze thought of us	I thought you were single?

Considering Mom's Offer, Sherri Takes a Hike

Is that a deer?	Don't do it, Sher	Her favorite footbridge	We'll kill each other	Forgot my Yeti
If we have a showroom, Mom, maybe	Ugh, Mom	Quit in two years, max	What if that's not a deer?	Partners, but Mom will always decide
What if it's not my dream	The whole thing in writing	**"Marie & Sherri Festo, Interior Designers"**	When do deer leave their moms?	Means well
I love you, Mom	Do deer daughters bite their deer moms?	It's not like Mom's happy	Trees don't *know* know, but they know	But Mom, you never
Deer work with other deer in the same office, kind of	Quit in a year, if	Durnit	You're always forgetting something, Sher	Paying Mom back

Jewish Christmas Eve Bingo

Wonton Soup (no one really likes it)	For once, can we not	The kids do a Yellow Brick Road march to the car	Your father has written a little poem	Shrimp with lobster sauce
This is the best	The girlfriend has invited him to Mass	Cousin ____, you know	Big kitchen love (shouting)	On the wall: "You will be happy when you are free"
We decided not to tell him	Lucky Numbers: 3, 11, 18, 51, 53	**We're different**	Whatever you do, don't say that name	So we have some news
Knicks hat, hoodie, leather jacket	The kids are going to the ten o'clock	Who ever heard of a little cancer?	Seven minutes of snow, the soft air, flakes on the eyelids	Anyone for decaf?
The unanswered phone	Your grandmother would have loved this	Stepping outside when the movie's over and time has stopped	Moo shu pork (not enough plum sauce)	Dessert in front of the TV

That Time Her Top Came Off

This isn't about her body. Or her shame which is also her pride, but more about new ways of thinking about bodies—and of course, the ocean, and the delight a body feels in the water.

We have come to understand that memory is mostly imagination.

That time the wave, the next wave, and then the really big wave all seemed to merge into one wave, although when the waves merge there's a kind of internal collapsing.

That time she half-turned and swallowed water with an unexpected gulp.

There was the frothy surf. So much mystery just below the surface, the teeming of life.

Someone will find the red bikini top on the beach tomorrow, in the washed-up algae, very early in the morning, someone collecting shells—someone with a mesh bag, the shells intended for a glass bowl on a glass coffee table. Will that person pick up the red bikini top and hold it in the air for a moment, dangling the surprise between two fingers? There's a sense of privacy or decorum, and a slight crinkling around the mouth, the red bikini top not an undergarment, but worn intimately, on the skin, by a stranger.

It's not about who sees.

In other countries, okay.

It's a little bit about what she's learned, and how an individual response in its variations can move through history in a moment. Her arm across her chest in an X of embarrassment and propriety, but then she doesn't care.

The red bikini top nowhere. Her laughter, her joy.

Hooping at the Y

"Step-back Steve"	Gotta start running more	Bobby's all about the deal	Taping it won't help	Rosie will beat on you
Who's she looking at?	The little guy draining 3s	Once, Laettner dropped by	Foul!	Wallet, ring, phone, keys
Left ankle	Rosie benchwarmed at Union	**Old and not**	The smelly realtor with the Tesla	Make the other Bobby go to his right
The mom from the pool with her hair in a towel	Box out!	Tuesdays	Left knee	Jesus, Rosie
Bobby's getting a divorce	Right shoulder	Box out, guys	Bobby's all elbows	Foul shots for next

Cut Thumb Bingo

It's not so bad	The two seconds before the bleeding starts	It was the other thumb in the bike wreck	That's it for paper towels	Jesus, maybe I love Sam
Hey, Siri, cancel Tuesday bowling	It's bad	The nasty smile of a cut	This is not *All Things Considered*	Why won't it stop?
I love Sam. I'm bleeding, but I love Sam!	Damn, not on the keyboard	**First time cooking for Sam**	That inhaled *hsssss*	Hey, Siri, I cut my thumb
Is that bone?	Shit, shit, shit, shit	No, Sam, I won't quit McKinsey	In the sink, the swirling pinkness	Sam, Sam, wham, ham, Sammy, Sammy, Sam
Hey, Siri, when is it blood loss?	What a color	To find the body, follow the drops	Got some on the rice	Crying already from the onions

Meeting Someone Once for Five Seconds

Imagine a woman who has come to a cabin two days ago. Not everything is put away yet; there are boxes stacked along one wall, all of them still closed, four or five that have been marked *Assorted*, the ones that will frustrate her getting settled. There are other boxes she didn't get to mark. The cabin's in a little clearing through a tree break, ruts in the road that worsen in winter, a local farmer paid to mow the field with his tractor, and he does, but it's hard to know how often. He mowed before she arrived, but only because she called.

The news in the country comes by wind: the world here is the weather. Because the wind goes and comes at the same time, and that's a kind of time that's always simultaneous, time becomes rich. Feels deeper. The scent of cedar in the wet morning arrives so strongly on the wind, the smell seems a burning.

Let's say she has a sister who lived in the cabin last year and planted a garden, sweetly muscled among the river rocks she laid by the south side of the house, ferns and pachysandra and a climbing rose that didn't thrive, and there's a dormant vegetable patch waiting for chicken wire. We're saying it's March—no, it's April. Yes, April. If she stays long enough, the woman plans to grow vegetables: carrots drilling down in the dark, and squash blossoms bursting like music that stays and then fades, and individual tomatoes sun-blushed and round. She'll put in the fence to keep out the rabbits, who know where to go, and stake the wire against the groundhog's tunneling through her hopes. The groundhog who is a nightmare, in the dark. She might even run the fence high, because of the deer.

On the third night a fox can be heard barking. Why?

It's an area with trout streams, where the fish seem to swim without moving in the riffles and eddies, wanting and having.

On the fourth morning, the wind shifts, the weather coming straight down. In the misty rain at the edge of the difference between woods and road, she sees a form that looks human, or only a combination of shadow and foliage.

We're saying her money won't run out, she has money, and now she's even living rent-free in her family's cabin built by a great-great uncle—although it's more likely he just bought it, family stories being stories. She's not very woodsy, in truth. We're saying she decided to tell only three people. She's healthy; that's important. We don't have to imagine her being sick.

She mostly reads biographies, and she did bring a few, and she has her tablet. And there are always puzzles wherever her sister has been.

The woman puts in a call to the satellite company. She isn't sure when they'll come; right now her appointment's three weeks away; everything is on hold, even here. The big living room windows are of course a kind of show, one that's slower than she's used to watching, with slight changes each day, and that's fun in a small way, for now. But she wants more action; she wants the fox to come, or the deer at dusk, or even a bear. Is it bear country? That seems possible, but it wasn't in the plan for her, or for what we wanted together, when we started all this.

Between us, we're trying to think about her, to stay focused on her needs, not ours: escape, solitude, loneliness, peace, shelter, a physical life, a return to her body and senses, her own judgement, limits, or even a neighbor who baked a pie. We imagine she hasn't had a vacation for two years at least, it's been so long, she works too much. We picture her with a roommate who has a friend who needed a place to stay, and the woman agreed and gave up her room for the summer, and now the rent on the apartment's paid, and even though her side gig has dried up, she'll be fine for a few months on salary and remote, or even just living off her savings on the cheap. It's all too dangerous at home.

We like drama in other people's lives. The move to the country should be a move to get away from a crisis, some emotional peril she's in, to flee a disaster, ditch a bad man/good lover. We want her to be choosing the cabin as refuge. We want her problems to be her own, not ours—not a worldwide thing, definitely not the unimaginable. We want her morning walks to mean something. But there's also the possibility that the difference between her city life and her country life will precipitate a dramatic shift, decisions that create tension, that she's here to risk a life beyond what she knows.

This is how I see people I don't know, and maybe you do too. The person you said *Excuse me* to at the farmer's market upstate, when you went for a drive because you had to, yes, you needed to get out—she's the woman we have imagined.

Because she's real, now.
Because you needed to get to the country, too.
Because, now, this is her life. We have imagined it together.
The unimaginable imagined.
Because I was there and I saw you, and when she said *That's okay*, as she stumbled too close to you, and then too close to me, we three were together.
Togetherness is a kind of strangeness.
Did you feel it? Was it okay? I hope so.

A September Wedding, Not Hers

Open bar	The groom's brother reaching for a tissue	No thanks, not since college	Balloons on the ceiling like wedding guests	How to trust a strapless bra
"Sharing a bathroom? No." - Maggie	Wanting something else	The leaves all red and gold like wedding guests	Love is love	That Queen Bey song, you know, "All the single ladies..."
Greg will never make enough	Augie from upstairs	**The vows**	Is Tino here?	The desserts on the buffet like wedding guests
The vows like hummingbirds	Fuck it	Mom liked Greg, of course	Rose petals in the aisle like wedding guests	Overheard: "Honey, I'm ovulating"
Imagine Greg here, ha	All the cute shoes like wedding guests	"Marry You," Bruno Mars	A basket of condoms in the ladies'	It seems real

John Flattery, Philosopher-Handyman

John Flattery is finally painting his kitchen. In aisle six of the big box store, the machine mixing the paint makes three sounds at once, each a thought. One sound sounds like a mechanical tide, geologic, steady and underground. Another sounds like someone's teeth rattling in a jar—that's the sound that bothers him. Then there's the banging, metal inside of metal, a hammering followed by random strikes, unpredictably, like when he was a boy hammering to be a man.

Aristotle writes, "The soul never thinks without an image." John Flattery thinks that his soul thinks more because he's watching the news all the time. He feels that same idea to be true, too. John Flattery is watching and feeling—and so, is his soul thinking? So many people suffering: so much injustice. The world was in lockdown, and now everyone's killing each other. He should stop reading Aristotle.

Maybe the soul and the self are the man, most of him, anyway, and the face he wears is his personality.

What he wants rolls in his mind, a swirling amalgamation. He can feel the mixing. It's amazing what the human ear and mind can process, or turn into a thought.

He has no image for his soul. His soul cannot think by itself, or imagine itself. But there is a soul.

Home through the fly-buzz of an Ottawa summer, windows down—the best part of shopping is driving with the stuff he gets. When John Flattery arrives home, the work will be what he has imagined: outlets taped and ceiling rolled, the sheen of the clean surface, the leftover stink, the room wet and new. Just the idea that he can imagine means he has an image of something, right? He can imagine his kitchen, for example.

But first there's a moment to be expected, when he pops open the big can of paint, and the swirls on the top have separated into different viscosities, colors floating, needing to be stirred together, and that's like the soul of John Flattery, a different idea of a soul.

John Flattery in the paint department of the big box store, choosing colors, the most important decision, living with what he imagines. Right. He'll do the ceiling in "Amazing Grey," and accent it with "Glamour."

Lilly's Bird Bingo

No, you are	The egg Lilly had to carry for health class last year	When Sophia laughed Dr. Pepper out her nose	What's the bird the other birds hate?	Bird school, bird parents, bird boys, bird hair, bird hips
Shit on Dad's bike helmet	When Lilly and Sophia got high and made tweet jokes and flapped their arms	Eleventh grade's a prison	Owl silhouette on the sliding glass door	The dead bird Lilly kept in the Forever 21 shopping bag
Sophia won't get the dodo tattoo too	Lilly wants hollow bones	**Love, *love*, the flock and swoop at dusk above the strip mall**	What's it called if you don't eat birds?	Horny-thol-ogy, hahaha
Is it better to have been a bird in a previous life...	It's just a thing, so shut up	Shocker: birds smell	What is Sophia's problem?	Dreams are birds
At Lew's party, Lilly Sharpies feathers on her arms	Pecking = boring	Sophia's beady bird eyes when she's mad	...or to be a bird in the next life?	

Community Garden Bingo

Townhouse	With work, the mind learns the body	Cute shorts	I think she's reading my email	Winning at something
Elder care	Do they know about us?	A slower dream	Hose with a leak (metaphor)	I never hit Reply All for just that reason
Creepy Hat Guy	Hose too short (sadness)	**Sunshine & water**	The soul of a growing thing	Your shirt's misbuttoned
Let's take my car	Biting into the strawberry (visions)	Sisters	Meet me at 4:30, and we'll go	If a building wanted to be something else
Running for office	Not since Rita died	A different daily experience of time	After dark, scattering his ashes	Shared governance (hope)

Trees

When at last he goes somewhere aside from picking up his groceries, he drives to the woods by the reservoir, bringing his mother's Minolta, the one Mom used on her "little trips," an old-school camera, film and all. Because Mom liked to take pictures of trees, and Mom just died.

If only a picture would capture what someone felt in the presence of each tree, what he felt, then who we are would be visible in the picture.

It's weird how remembering requires practice, and forgetting is part of remembering too, which makes them the same, almost.

If he knew a couple of things more, like about life, for example, he might not feel like he doesn't know where to fly now, and he's just flying around on the wind of feelings.

There's a tree so tall it seems to be standing on one leg, it looks wrong, there's no way it stays upright. Perhaps someone else would be wowed by that tree, how impossible it seems, but mostly he's just worried.

There's a tree too wide to see. Not really, of course, because all he has to do is back up enough, but when he does that, he can't get the canopy in the frame, he's too far away. So to see the tree and the canopy, or try to, he steps forward again. But that's impossible, no more big tree, no magic distance.

There's a tree that seems to move without a breeze. The leaves up there at the very top shiver and turn with the wind. The temperature must be different in the air up there. But the tree is always moving, just not down here. One side, or some, or many: now the leaves at the top on the other side are already shivering, and they turn, but then they stop and other leaves move again. The same group, or gathering, never moves twice: leaves aren't the same, even when they're the same leaves. That's a cool idea, the infinity part of it all.

What was the thing about Mom and pictures of trees? She must have identified. But the tree that looks most like a person is the fourth tree, and it's a mess. Trying to rearrange itself, to fix something; it seems restless, like it's going out to a party even though it's never going anywhere. Waving around, fiddling with its hair. That wasn't Mom, who was always together, at least until her last few days.

If only the picture in his head would be the picture the camera takes, something right to put in a shoebox.

Every tree has so many secrets, he thinks. All of these thoughts, for example. He knows he's feeling sad, and trying to see what sadness is. Or trying to see Mom.

He shoots the whole roll before heading home, hoping one shot will show Mom at the edge, a swallow that isn't in the picture anymore.

YOUR TURN

Jackie's Breakup Cupcakes Bingo

				Sue'll shit herself
Texting is so 2024				I don't hate Sue
Hah, Sue!		**Your message here**		
	Slightly bigger Little Debbies		www. breakupcupcakes. com	
			"Delivering the goods to the bads"	

Birthday Pony Bingo

				How much?
Rhonda would never have done this				Gaw, that smell
		Poop		
			He's choking!	
		Please don't rain		

Luis the Greeter Bingo

	Hello, mothers, welcome			Uh-oh, drunk girls
Wait, that drunk girl, that's		**Sell the smile**		
				Theatre degree
Please leave your			Hello, toilet paper	

Maya Sees a Moose

	That's no Clydesdale			
F-150 XXXXLT				But on Maple Lane?
		Then the moose sees Maya		
			Phone's dead	
	Nice Moosie Toosie			

Clean the Fridge Bingo

	"A box of circubits and boltheads." -William Cullen, 1747			
Hardened egg goo			It was your turn	
		What's this?		
But I love you				
				No, Gill will never

While on His Dinner Break, Martin Finishes Reading *The Glory of Augustus Caesar*

Antony's men drowned at Actium, blubbity blub. Martin tries not to see them as real people, lashed to their oars, going down; that's the part of history that hurts to read. In all the books he likes, people die. Which is hard to take because most people are okay, except the jerks and the racists. Like Julio on salads, he's okay, even that hostess, the sorority one. She works hard.

Martin's the kid in the kitchen with every suck job, the dorkiest suck job worker in the house. Which means he's scrubbing out the burned bits of honeyed baklava on the half-sheets, alone in the dish room where the radio is cranked to a shock jock urging some dude go get a vasectomy. Richie runs the radio, so it's either that or the news—or same difference, the thought making Martin giggle, the news as a dick joke.

On a wire shelf in the pantry, a platoon of oils in shiny green bottles glows, soldiers lining up, and on the floor, the beans do nothing in a big bag, each bean alike and different. Just waiting. Fish gleam one-eyed at Martin, on ice in their rubber tubs, who knows what they knew. He follows the prep list or he gets screamed at: Martin hits the walk-in for the onions, big-ass pearls in a burlap bag, because Chef needs a puttanesca.

Martin believes that wars are won or lost before they're fought, and some jobs suck. Antony's troops were already decimated by malaria as they waited for Octavian's navy to arrive, Cleopatra was no help, and Delius betrayed them all. Antony was dope, but at Actium he only had those useless quinqueremes—since a quinquereme, designed for ramming and plated with bronze at the bow, cool-looking, has no chance against a deadly smaller ship. Still the ballistas were so baller, the catapult jobbies that jacked boulders at the sailors on the deck, flattening Antony's men, *ka-zing, smush.* Martin loves the action scenes. He's got a replica ballista on his shelf at home.

Thinking about Actium, and how the book ended, and chopping vegetables; scrubbing down Chef Jeannie's workstation; hosing the slip mats and then the floor after close; scrubbing every surface; wiping; counting in his head when he's anxious, *97, 98, 99,* and if he has to, starting again, *0, 1, 2.* Martin feels different when a book ends. It's like time, only not the time we're living, not minutes or seconds, but time counted in other units, ones we don't know.

Martin's turning twenty-two next Tuesday. Recovery's going well. So he's only one-third of the way to death, or better yet, a quarter. He's getting to death slower. Yes, Dina's right, he should go back to school in the fall. Not just school, he says to the stock pot, to the big hole where the soup will be, like a universe the hole's so big, his whole head could go there. School and a girlfriend. Time to do something about himself, before he drowns in battle.

Suzie's Bedtime Bingo

Blinkie the Bunny loves Caw-Caw the Crow, and I drawed them on my easel	No, Daddy	Bunnies have extra feelings	Once Blinkie found a hole in the sky and went in	Caw-Caw eats garbage—icky garbage!
(Change the subject)	Blinkie hates when I go to Kiddie Kare, Daddy	The stars in Blink Land sound like popcorn	I miss Miss Naima	Blinkie's extra good at being extra happy, right?
Where did Miss Naima go?	Blinkie the Bunny nose kiss!	**Meltdown**	(Dr. Saunders says don't change the subject)	Blinkie is really good at her letters
Crows are bad but Caw-Caw is a good crow	(Change the subject)	Miss Naima has an angry friend like Gramps	Daddy, what's a hot flash?	Miss Naima says I'm very smart
It's not Blink Land, it's Blink Town!	Miss Naima still loves you, Sweet Pea	Sam bit Reggie	(Stay positive)	I love oranges most

Yard Sale Bingo

Put that down	Some fucking neighbor you are	Is it 18 karat?	Grilled cheese and tomato soup at Tony B's	We're not buying furniture, Dad
Dad, where's your wallet?	Ashtrays	Can I, can I, can I, can I, can I, can I, can I, can I, can I, can I, can I, can I, can I	Hey, next door put out a table	What's this for?
You're not on the permit	Be first	**Make an offer**	Dad, over here	Eight shower curtains
Never flash the cash	Dad, don't	Not an original	Man, Randy Thompson's pissed	Be last
Seven greasy spatulas	Fistfight!	Wait, Dad, you sold what?	Are those hamster ashes?	No price tag

A Minimal Supersymmetric Standard Model of the Universe

It's physics: everything's a string. I know, because I went to the hardware store, up and down the aisles and aisles of twine, and fishing line, and cord, and hemp. Polypropylene, nylon, sisal. Twist ties, zip ties. Cotton thread and silk thread on the shelves in Crafts. Measuring tapes and two different kinds of rope swings, one with coils and the other slipknots; one with a bench seat, the other a loop.

So I went outside: contrails. So I closed my eyes: rivers, wakes, and riptides.

I knew you were angry, and what could I do.

If I could see the invisible, then the invisible could be something. Conversations like ribbons, and feelings like buried power lines, don't dig here, and what I was feeling at breakfast with you has been following me all day, like the slow trail of memories of a slug on the brick walk.

I have tied a string around my pinky finger, to remember. People get married with strings around their wrists for luck.

Later, there will be aisles and aisles of stars, phantasmagorical strings of party lights, impossible streamers across the sky.

I will come back to you, because you are on the other end of the string I am.

Evelyn in Finance, Abdul in Logistics

Let's not start with complicated	OMG, new guy's name is Fred Éclair	7:56 a.m. I hear you in the elevator	Never date a coworker	Do you roller-skate?
Cookies?	I liked me more when you knew me less	Never date a coworker	Harrison knows	"Stupidity is also a gift of God…" -Mother Maria Su
Fine, Friday, but that's the last time	Really?	**I got you a present**	Let's switch to Gmail	Great bathroom sex
It's too soon to get me a present	Alexa, what rhymes with oh fuck?	Look, it's not like you know me	"The greatest gift…is that you can make creation infectious…" -Skrillex	Never date a coworker
Prosecco?	Never date a coworker	Life ain't a romcom, Snuggle Wump	I love presents	Did you hear about Khaira in HR and Reply All?

Rick's Road Rage

Predictable	Good thing Cara's not here	"You need to keep your emotional gates open, Rick"	Missed	To hell with the 403
Now!	Everyone, since Covid	Do it, Rick	Cara always says	Left lane, c'mon
Could you please	A gun wouldn't be a good idea	**Asshole!**	Signal, damn it	Even when she's not here, Cara
Cara's never going to	Pass, ha! then brake	It's not about work	Geezer	It's their turn to pull over and count to 20
Speed up, speed up, speed up, speed up, speed, speed, speed up, speed	Anders can stuff himself	Breathe	One of those	Work sucks

In Defense of Solitude

If I were a truck and I made my last delivery, I would like how complete I am. Done, done, done.

If I were a road that ended at the sunrise where the new houses ran out of money in the spangly dew, I would have a place to rest, unbothered.

If I were the separate thing that is a tree, and still belong.

If I were myself, back then, but with what I know now. Come to the table, my mother would say. Put down your crayons, stop smashing together your little army men, stop staring into those words. Each of us belongs, my mother would say. We're all immigrants in this country, my mother would say. Of course, not the Indians. Go ask your grandmother.

If I were a roller coaster I would have fun, *weeeee.*

If I were a fountain I would be pretty, *ahhhh.*

Why are you so quiet, my mother would say. Why are you always so awfully moody. Why are you so goddamn moody.

If I were the book I would close the book, and inside the book, in me, I would be safe.

If I were the music I would sneak through the drapes into people's lives, happy.

You're sitting there like your father, my mother would say.

High-Rise Window Washer Bingo

Snap the helmet snap	$75K	People in their tiny lives	Twisted	New kid on crane
That one dude who used to make goose noises	Jesus!	Cloud faces	Dream of a trailer in the desert	If lightning
Clip check	Bosun's chair	**Wind**	Fuck was that?	Flapping ear flap
Wave back	When the bough breaks	Never check the weather	Roof bolt	People are raisins
Tissues	Rope check	*squeee geeeeeee skrtttt*	A foreman named Worm	Cleat check

Tim the Weather Guy's Personal Forecast

Airspace, winds, clouds, tides	TV's real too	Green screen hiccups	Sure, I know you. So?	Anger Management
Those of you downtown, don't count on making it to Friday	The same	Whoa, that's a terrifying air mass	Agoraphobic	Decaf = Death
Tall caramel soy latte	Bailey's Insta says she's single	**Just keeping shit together**	The weather isn't personal, the weather isn't personal, the weather isn't	That sun'll fry your eyebrows right off
Dude cut the line	37° and raining	Look, no one got hurt yet	The same	The NASDAQ hires meteorologists
The same	The fuck you say I swore on air	It's just coffee, Slick	Makeup melt	Stay underground, folks

=

The way the two women walk six feet apart, one on the sidewalk and the other in the empty street = the way the body and the soul walk together in the afterlife.

Chatting = remembering = saving.

How one of the women gestures with her hands when she speaks, shaping the air into invisible shapes = ideas in the afterlife, shapes made of air.

= is a statement of equivalence without value.

The way the other woman, the one whose body seems still even as she speaks, is more introspective, more of a listener = how a person in life encounters the unknown, if they're lucky, to speak and listen to the unknown.

When the space between the two friends on their night walk = intimacy, they have achieved their goal, which is not to let the particulars of existence determine personhood. Not to let being together = not being allowed to be together.

Six feet apart ≠ six feet under.

Walking in the street where there are no cars = a feeling from childhood, from summertime.

Walking on the sidewalk with her friend walking in the street = a feeling of maturity, being ever-so-slightly in charge, that first moment of control, an inflection point of adulthood.

Both women laugh when they get to the cul-de-sac. One woman has an especially great laugh, with a bit of a bark to it, and the other swallows her laugh a little, but laughs so well at everything. They both know this is funny, as they consider without speaking whether to circle the loop in the same formation, or to change their walking arrangement as they walk back home, and who will walk where. The spontaneity of their laughter, and the eye contact held for longer than the laugh lasts, makes them stop for a moment, smile to one another, and understand without comment that this = the seen and the unseen.

This is the luck they share, when their differences = their affections = living.

Union Station Bingo

Suitcase loses a wheel	One-way ticket	Thirty-one adults in red and blue overalls	If only he had apologized	He won't post that picture, right?
Having just called your lover by your dead dad's name	No time for a bite	It's only a sprain	These lives, and all of their opening credits	The two-story escalator doesn't stop on Two (you learn)
Seven huge guys in camo, open carry	In the great soaring vault fly the 19th century ghosts	**Now**	Suddenly, your sister	Reading *Civilization and Its Discontents*
It's never Daylight Savings Time until it's Daylight Savings Time	Closed for cleaning	The unhoused	If only you had apologized	Pews (there's an Amish family)
Fourteen fourteen-year-olds sprawled, on their phones	He took the cash from your wallet (you don't know yet)	Space is Time	The hotel seemed sketchy	You're also the bird who can't get out

The Lumber Mill at Night

He's fifteen, and flung asleep, arms above the head, like he's hollering hallelujah, which he'd never do, when his mother enters the room to turn off the godawful sounds, the drums and guitars cranked, the Grief Knuckles' "vocals" shaking the apartment walls. If he wakes now, she'll be caught—standing here knowing better, again, because she does. Which doesn't mean she should say so.

How the hell does he sleep through that? Music on, music off, he's not going to wake up for another ten hours at least. Also, he's nicer to her when he's asleep. She could just stand here until he's twenty, just knock him out over and over.

The kid snores like her ex. The music and the snoring's an awful combination, like a fucking lumber mill, she thinks, which makes her remember the lumber mill out on Chester Country Road, from when she was a kid. Which she visited with her dad.

She turns the music down, closes her eyes, to let the memory be.

Her dad was building a shed he didn't need. He took his daughter—why?—he brought his daughter to the lumbermill, the daughter he wouldn't let near his tools.

On the shop floor, there was a bandsaw and plane, a whine and a racket, and the too-sweet smell of sawdust. Thirty feet clear of the loading dock, men in safety goggles were smoking and laughing—it was dangerous to work the mill. A forklift beeped by a sagging U-Haul trailer, as another pickup backed in.

And then out front, a row of trucks and trailers in the lot, bumper stickers shouting dumb stuff. In Areas 1 and 2 by the gate, sprinklers doused the mountains of stacked timber, aging the wood, or just pouring water because of everyone's fear of fire.

Her dad bought stuff. Or he didn't? What were they doing there? Why?

They went out for breakfast together. Eggs and Canadian bacon in his usual booth where her father waved to his fishing buddy the cop, who also came for the morning rush, where the men sat down to a coffee the waitress had already poured.

The kid will never know his grandfather. That's okay.

She could blink three times, or even bang a couple of frying pans together, and the kid wouldn't stir, dreaming in the grip of the Grief Knuckles and hormones. She could give him a haircut, she could steal all of his left shoes, she could rearrange his dresser drawers, she could Crisco the floor, slather Icy Hot in his underwear. She could draw a dick in Sharpie on his forehead, like in that movie, take his picture and post it, tag his girlfriend, blame his dad. Which all made her understand that she couldn't, that she wasn't a guy, to hell with all that.

What it would be like for the kid and his mom to get their lives back? Where Tyler wasn't his father ever. That's what she would actually choose: Tyler becoming a man free of men.

Don't Hate Your Daddy Bingo

Have a song to sing to yourself	Ask him for advice, even if	Read Tennessee Williams	That time he tried to hit the janitor with a mop handle	What if there's a Judgment Day
Change the subject	Father-in-law's worse	He laughs	COVID-19	At the football game together, you take a knee
Help elect a candidate under the age of fifty	That time he meant to compliment you	**Old people can change**	Read Sylvia Plath	He takes a fish hook out of your leg
Marry a person more likeable than you	Read *Notes of a Native Son*	Take a fish hook out of his leg	Say yes, and don't	Change the subject
When he mono-logues on the phone, step out and ring your own doorbell: "Gotta go, someone at the door!"	Mom was worse	Here's permission to	Never say what you really care about	When he gets snippy, treat with food

Squirrel at the Bird Feeder Bingo

Mom at her window, chain-smoking	"A family divided has never enough nuts" -Proverb	But who eats the seed at night?	To love to hate	Mom bites her nails
Swing, feeder, swing, feeder, feeder swing, swing	Greasing the pole's an option, Mom	Mom's cigarette butts in the sink	The nuts undug are the trees to be	Napping on purpose, when the nurse comes
Do birds think?	So many diseases	**Woo-woo! Getoffathere!**	A cat's an option, Mom	"If your father"
Hate's not for free	"The little yellow birdies—they're like candies"	Tuesdays when the nurse comes	Claws for hands	That one's looking at me
"A squirrel, opposeth to Man, shews peril by immobility." -Dr. Arthur Winston, 1753	Move the feeder, Mom	"If I were a squirrel, I'd be nice"	The nurse doesn't bite, Mom	A test designed to fail

The Past or the Future

The dog's dug another hole and squeezed under the fence again to leave me, naked, calling her name from the back porch and trying not to spill my coffee (hot, hot) and squinting into the dark yard, dazed, as I poke with my tongue the tender spot in my mouth where the bubbling mozzarella from the bad pizza burned me, and then you kissed it better.

Out there belongs to the dog: tea towels she dragged from the kitchen, the chewed-off heel of a dead pair of pumps, that shitty plastic bucket she carries around like it's prey, the bones buried to thwart thieves. Still, she's all about escape.

The dog sat on her ass and stared at the bed and whined, so I rose from you, shiny with you, and let her out.

The dog loves you more than she loves me, which she and I understand, and she's never had sex, for which I have meant to apologize, because it's sad for an animal.

The past is a good dog. Or the future. Or the future is a bad dog. Then there's time panting, panting like a clock.

The dog's favorite bad dog game is to jump on the laundry I hang on the line, splatting her muddy paws on it, growling with glee, wrestling my hard work to death.

Okay, so once in a dream there was a planet owned and run by dogs, and I lived there in a fenced yard, and I could run really fast but I had no thumbs, and nothing to hold onto without thumbs. Four legs are fun, but being trapped is not.

It's creepy, I know, but I'm slowly trading places with the dog. Escape, I think. Bad dog.

Twins

Back home together with Braden to take care of things, Julie climbs out her mom's window to lie back on the rough roof of the porch. She has a straight shot up at the moon from here, between thinning branches of the oak, and like the moon, Julie cannot sleep.

Among the memories on their hangers in the closet, Julie found an old pair of overalls that fits well enough if she wears a sweatshirt inside. Overalls are good for April, when the sky wants to suck her back into her childhood. Plus it's nippy out here, and she knew it would be—she knew from twenty-three years ago, when she was eleven, and started lying on the roof at night. Even as a kid, Julie learned what to wear, practical she is, our Julie, Mom says.

Only Beast, her Mom's bad gray calico, is awake. Hissing atop the bookcase in the hall as Julie came back from refilling her water glass, that crazy-ass cat. So she hissed back at him, the cat who yesterday pissed on her laid-out nightgown. The cat who has always been a bad cat, still feral, rescued or not; a bad cat is a bad cat.

It's better out here, the air less stuffed with smells, and Julie doesn't feel alone, since Braden's in the house, sleeping in the sewing room. Because they're twins, their awareness of each other stretches out, touching, like the moonlight going everywhere, and especially when they've spent time talking. Twins ramp up. Although she assumes that Braden's as talked out as Julie is, all this talk about Mom, what's next for Mom.

Thinking of him connects them: she can hear him cough, get up, cough, clomp down the hall to the bathroom.

Julie stays where she is on the roof: no reason to talk again. A person could live out here, eating the stars, living off of them.

Maybe thinking about Julie woke him up.

Then Braden's back, and he steps into her room. He's half asleep, sleep-stumbling to her window. She starts to say something, stops.

He closes the window, locks it, locking her out. Of course. Twins.

The Wrongs and Rights of Gracie Matsusoki

Become an ultrasound technician	Did I blow it?	Stop, just stop	Wanting, needing, deserving, wanting	Like you never, Dr. Waters
Cat person	If there are no clouds, the sun is just the sun	Become a graphic designer	Anal sex	Stop Googling him
Combat boots, LBD, Yankees hat	Dang, his brother died	**And when we're together**	A ramen truck in the rain	*Bad Men Are No Good* by Tina Syla, Ph.D., MSW
Making this Bingo card isn't helping, Dr. Waters	*Know Your Love Button* by Eliza Shleegal	That summer waiting tables in P-Town	Fish tank person	Pilates suck
He'll leave his wife	Costa Rica was fun	Plant person	Sexting	It's not like that, Dr. Waters

Erik Reads *Art News*

Painting asks the questions	Envy, bad	Self-esteem	$	Less caffeine tomorrow
No love in grad school	Credit cards are for losers anyway	A leaf	Sex is color	Life isn't painting
Get fired on Monday	"Don't let them tame you." – Isadora Duncan	**But when the stuff goes together**	The F in MFA	Hockney stole that idea
Ding an sich	Thanks for the subscription, Mom	That guy? No way	Ask all of the questions every day	Wrong century
Oils smells	Solve it in the studio	A job on Airplane Mode	"Deepen the mystery." - Francis Bacon	Too much love in grad school

Ella's Letter to the Editor of the Universe

Someone has balled the clouds and thrown them into one corner of the sky—the clouds all together up there, and yet still moving this way.

Someone has sharpened the trees and jammed them in.

Someone has parked the cars with just the right amount of distance between them—and then one of the cars is parked too close, front and back. That's the car to worry about.

It's time to go, says the mourning dove. Where?

Someone makes us take the sidewalk, the longest way around the lawn.

What I have in common with other people is that we're different people.

Someone has put Beauty in the same aisle as Health Essentials.

It's not a moral universe.

Someone has used the human penchant for choice to justify hatred.

Someone has divided us. We agree to those divisions: you're over there and I'm over here, and we're not the same.

Rarely do we get the same ice cream twice. Despite quality control, and the consistency with which mixing and chilling and the addition of artificial flavors makes for taste-testing approval, despite unified branding concepts, despite the ice cream sitting squarely on the same shelf in frozen foods, the flavor's wrong. Not quite mint chip, when mint chip is why.

Someone keeps changing the technology, so that aging happens faster and lasts longer. The people who are aging faster are older than the younger people—and that's a feeling older people can take personally. Except in some other cultures.

It's true the people who keep changing the technology are young people.

If I were in charge, there would be no difference between the inside and outside. But someone else is in charge. Someone's out there.

Is it you?

Yours,

Ella

The Bridge

I carry my father on my back. He's not as heavy as he once was, even with his army boots on, the clunky leather ones he insisted on wearing, the army having been "a time" (although he was a prison guard who never saw action). His cap with the fuzzy earflaps is a good idea. Wearing the suspenders is also a good idea. When he developed a pouchy belly, suspenders made sense—and it turned out he was willing to wear them, which surprised us all. So, good: wear the suspenders.

We set out from his apartment. I take the stairs, even though it's seven flights down, because down's easy, plus I need to get into a rhythm and find my balance. Chin and cheek pressed to my neck, he's muttering instructions, but it's been a very long time since I have understood what he says. I don't care that he wants to be in charge. But I also don't understand what he's babbling about: could be he's hungry, or we forgot some crucial memento. He's all opinion these days.

At each landing, I give a little hitch, hoist him up again—because he kind of slides around as we go down. I don't want him to fall. And I will need to be comfortable.

The stairway in his building leads to the lobby, a glassed-in, two-story atrium brightened by skylights, with a pretty indoor fountain, the plumes jetting through long strings of coins that flutter and flip. Nice, for a building this size. I think the fountain convinced him to move here—he didn't want to leave the old house, for sure.

He's restless, I can tell, and he wants to stop, which is fine for now: it's early and I'm not in a hurry. I set him down on the floor. He holds both hands on the edge of the fountain and rocks a little, staring into the water where the wishing coins shimmer. I reach over and cup some water, splash my sweaty face, and my father looks at me, surprised, but he too reaches forward, and I palm a little water into his palms, and he splashes his face.

We're ready—or I am. I hoist him up.

There are arduous days and nights ahead, who knows how long the trip will take, no one ever says: forest after forest, a desert that's supposed to be especially challenging. Some have said there's a mountain range. I'm sure we'll encounter personal tests, trials I expect to be bested by, and for sure a few monsters along the way. We all find ourselves wanting. But if we're lucky, when we get there, if the season allows, we might find a sturdy boat to take us across the sea. And when we reach the bridge, perhaps I will be able to ease him down, and someone else will carry him the rest of the way, and I can turn back toward home.

All the Cell Phones Ring at Once

<table>
<tr><td>Look, look up,
look at one
another</td><td>Reaching for
her purse, the
anchorwoman</td><td>5:56 p.m.</td><td>Ruby's only
three</td><td>Hello?</td></tr>
<tr><td>"When, on the
other hand, the gods
purge the earth..."

-Plato</td><td>Which
government?</td><td>Check CNN</td><td>About whom
shall we think
to think?</td><td>Ruby loves
Peek-a-Zoo</td></tr>
<tr><td>Jesse Eugene
Russell, inventor
of the digital cell
phone (b. 1948)</td><td>Jalissa</td><td>Everybody
get down</td><td>4.30389.
/A8/spectral.
data/h</td><td>So hello from the
other side

- Adele</td></tr>
<tr><td>Ruby, Ruby, my
little Ruby Lee</td><td>Can anything
happen?</td><td>Save us all</td><td>Even her
shoulders are
shaking</td><td>Once it stops—</td></tr>
<tr><td>Day care was
always a mistake</td><td>Hey, Siri, are
you there?</td><td>The new camera
guy says
EMP</td><td>All of us</td><td>Hang on, Ruby,
I'm coming</td></tr>
</table>

Porch Swing Bingo

Egg moon	What's that pickup doing?	Only at night are we	Gun rack?	Nonstop cicadas
Pepsi and gin	Ping-Pong moon	Finally alive	The cicadas	Skin
His engine's running	A slo-mo moon	**Reaching out, and yes, holding hands**	Are there two people in that truck?	Better than
MAGA sticker	The cicadas	The eye moon	Skin	Must be the neighborhood patrol
Cicadas, cicadas, cicadas	At night, we can	The never lonely moon	Jeffrey wouldn't want	Priest moon

Notes:

For more information about Edwin S. Lowe, the inventor of Bingo:
https://thebiggamehunter.com/company-histories/e-s-lowe-toy-company/

"Feti's Border Crossing":

"Another barrier is the fundamentalism of monolingualism," writes Ngũgĩ wa Thiong'o in "The Politics of Translation: Notes Towards an African Language Policy," presented as the Neville Alexander Memorial Lecture at the Harvard Center for African Studies on April 19, 2016.

"Allison's Library Adventure":

In Kalynn Bayron's YA novel, *Cinderella Is Dead* (NY: Bloomsbury YA, 2020), the author reimagines the classic tale as a queer romance in a post-apocalyptic world.

"After School":

"Milo the Amazing" is a shoutout to Milo and Tock in *The Phantom Tollbooth* by Norton Juster (NY: Random House, 1961). Thank you, Uncle Nort.

"KB Meets Her Birth Mom":

내 딸 in Korean means "my daughter."

"Dr. Ozan Builds a Violin":

The comforts of the violin were well-known to a certain Mr. Holmes: "A sandwich and a coffee, and then off to violin-land, where all is sweetness and delicacy and harmony, and there are no red-headed clients to vex us with their conundrums." From "The Red-Headed League." Sir Arthur Conan Doyle. *The Complete Sherlock Holmes* (NY: Bantam Books, 1986).

"Music is not illusion, but revelation rather." Pyotr Ilyich Tchaikovsky, Letter to Nadezhda Filaretovna, December 5, 1977. Translation mine. https://en.tchaikovsky-research.net/pages/Letter_679.

As Yehudi Menuhin writes in his memoir, *Unfinished Journey: Twenty Years Later* (London: Fromm International, 1997), his 1742 Guarneri violin—nicknamed "The Lord Wilton"—was ideal for Brahms.

"First Day Bingo":

Mike Irimisha, author of *How to Succeed at Being You Without Knowing Who You Are* (Washington, D.C.: Market Books, 2013), is serving a five-year sentence for elder exploitation, wire fraud, and embezzlement.

Dr. Lucas Fjörlen was the first to identify the syndrome that bears his name, a condition remarkable for the misplacement of objects. One's favorite scissors, for example, might be found in the freezer; the AA batteries could show up in a soap dish.

"People Floating Away Bingo":

"Rashid" is a shoutout to the storyteller dad in Salman Rushdie's *Haroun and the Sea of Stories*, a wondrous example of real magic.

"Mickey Falls Asleep at Work":

Dr. Mehta Singh, pop psychologist, was briefly ambassador to the Republic of Suriname in the early 1980s, where he did his best work on dream interpretation.

"Dreamlover" was written by Mariah Carey and David Hall in 1993. The full lyrics of the passage heard by Mickey while dreaming are: "Dream lover, come rescue me (yeah) / Take me up, take me down / Take me anywhere you want to, baby now."

Dr. Arvina Hoolse is an eminent psychoanalyst working in Antwerp, whose reputation has spread almost entirely by word-of-mouth.

"The Strangeness of Knowledge":

The Kansas City, KS to Des Moines, IA Greyhound bus is operated by Jefferson Lines. Seats may not be reserved.

"César's Eye Exam":

Aarhuis Nomo's landmark work on vision and morphology, *See/Be* (London: Ex Libris Books, 1997), remains the standard in the field.

Clothing designer Gianni Versace (1946-1997) was known for the use of lettering on fabrics, especially on butts.

"Liza Rosen Sees Cyndi Lauper at the Walgreens":

In a 1995 interview with Martin Bashir of the BBC, Diana, the Princess of Wales, averred, "I would like to be the queen of people's hearts." https://www.pbs.org/wgbh/pages/frontline/shows/royals/interviews/bbc.html.

"She Bop" was written by Cyndi Lauper, Stephen Broughton Lunt, Gary Corbett, and Rick Chertoff. The 1984 song was once considered controversial for its forthright treatment of masturbation.

"Delilah Hates Chem":

H_2SO_4 is sulfuric acid.

10 KNO_3 +3 S + 8 C is the balanced reaction of gunpowder.

CH_3COOH is popularly known as acetic acid.

Ms. Paula Stagnitta was my second-grade teacher.

"Ireni and the Ghost":

As of this writing, the domain www.eulogy.com remains available for purchase.

"Car Crash Bingo":

Rihanna's 2007 "Shut Up and Drive" was written by Carl Sturken and Evan Rogers, and based on a song by the band New Order.

"Greek Diner Coffee Bingo":

According to Hesiod, Aphrodite, the goddess of love, gets her name from the "white foam" of her father's genitals tossed into the sea; thus she's "foam-born." Hesiod, *Theogeny*, 173.

"Coffee makes us severe, and grave, and philosophical," writes the great satirist Jonathan Swift in *Miscellanies* (1722).

Kalimera! means good morning in modern Greek.

"Jewish Christmas Eve Bingo":

The writing on the wall, "You will be happy when you are free," alludes to the Nazi slogan, "Arbeit macht frei," a phrase on the entrance gate at Auschwitz.

"Hooping at the Y":

The story includes a cameo by the former professional basketball player Christian Laettner.

"A September Wedding, Not Hers":

"Single Ladies (Put a Ring on It)" was written by Beyoncé Knowles, Christopher "Tricky" Stewart, and Terius "The-Dream" Nash. The song won a Grammy in 2009 for "Song of the Year." "Marry You" (2011) was written by Bruno Mars, Philip Lawrence, and Ari Levine.

"John Flattery, Philosopher-Handyman":

"The soul never thinks without an image," writes Aristotle in *On the Soul* (ca. 350 B.C.). Translation mine.

"Clean the Fridge Bingo":

William Cullen (1710-1790) was President of the Royal College of Physicians and Surgeons of Glasgow. He is credited with the invention of artificial refrigeration.

"Trees":

The story takes its inspiration from Susan Sontag's *On Photography* (NY: Penguin Books, 2010).

"While on His Dinner Break, Martin Finishes Reading *The Glory of Augustus Caesar*":

The biography referred to in the story's title is by Hardison C. Marks (London: Lieb Classics, 1959).

"A Minimal Supersymmetric Standard Model of the Universe":

The title of the story refers to an attempt in particle physics to correct the Standard Model's "naturalness problem."

"Evelyn in Finance, Abdul in Logistics":

Mother Maria Su was a missionary in Indonesia. Her lectures on abstinence and abstemiousness were known for their ardor, and for lasting four or five hours.

Skrillex, DJ and producer, was born Sonny John Moore in Highland Park, Los Angeles, in 1988. He is credited with popularizing brostep.

"Tim the Weather Guy's Personal Forecast":

The NASDAQ has a staff of meteorologists.

"Union Station Bingo":

In 1986, to free the birds living in the old Union Station in Washington, D.C., workers temporarily covered with black cloth a wide swath of the ceiling windows, turned off all of the building's interior lights, and then opened a twenty-by-twenty-foot square in the middle of the cloth. Most of the birds flew out. www.unionstation.org/d.c./birdsfreed.

Sigmund Freud's *Civilization and Its Discontents* (1922) famously opens with the phrase, "It is impossible to escape the impression that people commonly use false standards of measurement…and that they underestimate what is of true value in life."

"Pews in the Church of Time" alludes to a painting by Kristian Kristiansen, the great Norwegian Naturo-*Surrealisme* artist, that hangs in the ArtHus Gallery in Bergen, NO.

"The Lumber Mill at Night"

The Grief Knuckles are best known for their 2017 crossover deathcore release, *Bite-Fuck the Babysitter.*

"Don't Hate Your Daddy Bingo":

Notes of a Native Son is by James Baldwin.

"Squirrel at the Bird Feeder Bingo":

While Groucho Marx famously declared in 1931, "A family divided has never enough nuts," the phrase itself is thought to be an earlier American proverb.

The observation "A squirrel, opposeth to Man, shews peril by immobility" may be found in the early journal writings of Dr. Arthur Winston (1753), the "surgeon" who invented the inter-vascular straw.

"The Wrongs and Rights of Gracie Matsusoki":

Tina Syla's much-maligned self-help monograph, *Bad Men Are No Good* (NY: Delancey Books, 1999) spent 71 weeks on the *New York Times* bestseller list. Considerable disagreement exists regarding Syla's claim to have received either a PhD or an MSW. (To prevent legal entanglements, she is listed here as having both degrees.)

Eliza Shleegal's *Know Your Love Button* (L.A.: Silk Books, 1985) is in the process of being revised as gender-neutral.

"Erik Reads *Art News*":

"The job of the artist is to deepen the mystery"—attributed to the painter Francis Bacon—may have been first said by Georges Sand (the pen name for Amantine Lucile Aurore Dupin de Francueil).

"You were once wild here. Don't let them tame you." Isadora Duncan, *Isadora Speaks: Uncollected Writings and Speeches of Isadora Duncan*. (SF: City Lights Books, 1971).

"All the Cell Phones Ring at Once":

Plato writes in the *Timaeus,* "And when, on the other hand, the Gods purge the Earth…." (ca. 360 B.C.). https://plato.stanford.edu/entries/plato-timaeus/.

The hit song "Hello" (2015) was written by Adele Adkins and Greg Kurstin.

In 1992, Jesse Eugene Russell (b. 1948) received US Patent No. 5,084,869 for his "digital cellular base station."

Acknowledgements

The following stories have appeared in journals, often in earlier versions (with thanks):

The Academy of American Poets "Poem-a-Day": "Feti's Border Crossing," with an audio performance by twelve artists, recorded at the Virginia Center for the Creative Arts, July, 20, 2022. https://poets.org/poem/fetis-border-crossing.

Copper Nickel: "In Defense of Solitude," "People in Light and Shadow"

DIAGRAM: "The Past or the Future"

Fiction Kitchen Berlin (GDR): "Meeting Someone Once for Five Seconds"

Forum: "Squirrel at the Bird Feeder Bingo"

Heavy Feather Review: "Car Crash Bingo," "First Day Bingo," "Long Marriage Bingo" and "Union Station Bingo"

The Lincoln Review (UK): "How Phil Imagines the Afterlife"

Litro: "Ella's Letter to the Universe"

Lunate (UK): "Unemployment Benefits"

Necessary Fiction: "Speculative Fiction"

The New Flash Fiction Review: "=," "The Dragonfly"

The Opiate: "Janet and Her Soul," "The Plumber"

River Styx: "The Bridge"

Terrain.org: "Lilly's Bird Bingo"

Vestal Review: "John Flattery, Philosopher-Handyman"

Virginia Quarterly Review: "Change Your Life Bingo," "Community Garden Bingo," "Don't Hate Your Daddy Bingo," "Greek Diner Coffee Bingo," "High School Reunion Bingo," and "Jewish Christmas Eve Bingo"

"People in Light and Shadow" was nominated for a Pushcart Prize by *Copper Nickel.*

"Lilly's Bird Bingo" was nominated for *Best American Stories* by the editors of *Terrain.org.*

"Change Your Life Bingo," "Community Garden Bingo," "Don't Hate Your Daddy Bingo," "Greek Diner Coffee Bingo," "High School Reunion Bingo," and "Jewish Christmas Eve Bingo" were awarded the 2021 Emily Clark Balch Prize from the *Virginia Quarterly Review* for the best poems published in the journal that year.

"The Bridge" was awarded third place in the *River Styx* Annual Microfiction Contest, 2021.

"Unemployment Benefits" was awarded the Lunate (500) Prize for flash fiction, 2020.

"The Cuellos' Thanksgiving" appeared in *And If That Mockingbird Don't Sing: Parenting Stories Gone Speculative*, ed. Hannah Grieco. Alternating Current Press (Boulder, 2022).

With thanks to Davidson College, the Virginia Center for the Creative Arts, and Wildacres. With respect for the avidity of Bingo players, especially Norma Garcia and Mamie Lynds.

With thanks to the following editors, readers, and chums, for their gracious assistance and encouragement: Sandra Beasley, Shireen Campbell, Daniel Lynds, Michelle Dotter, Cynthia Hogue, Pam Houston, Jeff Jackson, Corey Marks, Gregory Pardlo, Eli "Parker" Parker, Sarah Perry, Kevin Prufer, Sundi Richard, Preston Witt, and Wayne Miller.

For Felicia, *te amo.*

About the Author

Alan Michael Parker is the author of fourteen books, including *The Committee on Town Happiness* and *Christmas in July*. His work has twice appeared in *Best American Poetry*, and been awarded three Pushcart Prizes and three Randall Jarrel Awards, as well as the Fineline Prize, the Lunate 500 Prize, and the Balch Prize. In 2021, he judged the National Book Award in fiction, and in 2024, the PEN/Faulkner Award in fiction. He is Houchens Professor of English at Davidson College, where he chairs the English Department. He has been called "a general beacon of brilliance" by *Time Out, New York.*